D1566764

Night in the Underworld

by
Mark Stephen O'Neal

This short story is loosely based on true events, and some names, places, events, and identifying details have been changed to protect the privacy of individuals.

ALSO BY MARK STEPHEN O'NEAL

The Root of All Evil
Frenemy
Blind Fury
Deception
Nefarious

1

There had been a steady May rainfall since the early afternoon on Friday, and the streets were beginning to flood. Rush hour traffic on Sibley Boulevard in Dolton, Illinois was at a virtual standstill, as the visibility was near zero, because the shower had morphed into a torrential rainfall. I had to swerve away from what looked like a small pond on the right-hand side of the street, in order to avoid potentially flooding my engine while on my way to the Walgreens on the corner of Woodlawn Avenue and Sibley Boulevard. The plan was to buy two Arizona green teas because they had the two-for-a-dollar special going on, and I needed to stay hydrated for the duration of the evening. I also wanted to grab a burger from the Rally's that was a few blocks west of the Walgreens, after I filled up my gas tank at the Food-4-Less grocery store.

My name is Red—I had been the only caramel-complected dude on my block with hair as reddish-brown as mine was back in the day, so the name stuck to me like glue. I had started driving for Uber in the Chicagoland area four months after my unemployment benefits and severance money ran out in a year's time, as I'd had no luck find a job earning the money that I was accustomed to making in the banking industry. However, being single had allowed me to be frugal and stretch out the money as long as humanly possible.

The job layoff had also been a blessing in disguise, even though I couldn't fully recognize it at first glance. My last day of employment at this check processing firm in the West Loop was December 10, 2013, and I was on my way to work after being on vacation for a week. I had used the last of my days because I couldn't carry them over into the next year, and that burned-out feeling I had a week prior was gone. There was nothing out of the ordinary happening on this particular day at first, as I made my way to Interstate 94—a two-minute ride from my apartment in Calumet City, Illinois. Traffic flowed steadily to downtown Chicago until I got to the Kennedy-Eisenhower split, so I exited the expressway at 22nd Street and Canalport Avenue to avoid the traffic buildup. I then drove northeast on Canalport Avenue to Canal Street, and I rode Canal Street all the way to the Apparel Center where I worked for over sixteen years as a sorter operator of my department for a financial services firm.

I routinely circled the perimeter, looking for free parking, and found a spot next to Jewel-Osco grocery store that was three blocks from the job. I remembered it being cloudy and briskly cool while I hastened toward the dock area of the building. The usual suspects were on break taking smokes, and I customarily greeted the security guard before heading to the elevator. There was usually a long wait for the freight elevator to come down to the basement—but not on that day. It came right down a few seconds after I pressed the button.

There was something strange in the air at that moment, but I couldn't quite put a finger on it. I rode the elevator alone up to the eighth floor and looked at my watch. It read 2:36 p.m. Damn, I was late again by six minutes, I thought. Being late was a bad habit that I'd developed over the last year—I had a good attendance record, but punctuality wasn't my strong suit. I had been going through the motions for years because I'd reached a point where I was unfulfilled at work and saw no future in staying with the company.

I got off the elevator and walked past the women's bathroom to my left toward my area to swipe in, and there was dead silence. We had been in the process of moving the entire department to the other side of the building on the eighth floor before I went on vacation, and the move was completed once I had gotten back. All the computers, supplies, and coworkers' personal belongings were gone, and all that remained within the area were the empty desks and cabinets, the empty racks where the checks were stored, and the obsolete DP-1850 check sorters that were shut down completely a month ago. My job had been phased out, and my company was moving in another direction. However, I had been training on the newer, slower check processing machines that were equipped to handle a much smaller volume of transactions and felt somewhat secure that my job was safe for the time being.

I subsequently scanned the entire office and couldn't find a single living soul, so I left the area to go to the other side where everyone else appeared to be. That was when I was met halfway down the hall by one of the first-shift bosses, and she requested that I follow her to one of the conference rooms in the vacant office. I sensed at that moment my services were no longer needed. The head of the department and a human resource administrator were waiting for me once we arrived in the conference room. The first-shift boss left, and the three of us had a closed-door meeting. I was then told that my services were terminated, the company was moving in another direction with the changing of technology within the firm, and that I had a severance package coming. They also said there was assistance available in finding another job, courtesy of the company, and they wished me good luck in my future endeavors.

The meeting had lasted ten, maybe fifteen, minutes or so—but who was counting? I shook both gentlemen's hands, gave the human resource guy my ID, and left the building without a personal escort. I'd witnessed dozens of former employees whisked out of the office as if they were common criminals threatening to shoot up the building because they had been fired, but I was able to leave with an ounce of dignity for having clocked in sixteen years of service. Or maybe they let me leave on my own accord because everyone else was safe and secure on the other side of the floor. Nevertheless, I didn't give it anymore thought after I made my descent to the first-floor lobby on the elevator.

My last day was just how I had envisioned it—no tears, no goodbyes from coworkers, and no regrets. I'm sure I was the talk of the office for a day at least, and I even got a text from my team leader wishing me well. I'm a loner who would shun any spotlight or fanfare, so my departure was the perfect ending to a solid but unspectacular career at my former place of employment.

I sauntered back to my car trying to digest what had just taken place. I wasn't angry, worried, or sad—surprisingly, I felt relieved and free. The thought of never having to darken the doorstep of my former employer gave me a sense of peace that I never experienced in my forty years of life at the time. I thought I could now apply for the jobs that offered the salary comparable to the lifestyle I wanted to live, because my severance package and unemployment benefits would allow me several months to be selective in my job search and put my degree in business administration to use. I left the downtown area and got on the southbound Dan Ryan Expressway. "Welcome to the first day of the rest of my life" was what I thought at that time.

Fast-forward slightly over five years later, and I was essentially my own boss in a sense while driving for Uber, because I can pick my own hours and days of the week when I worked. I had a great rating from my riders at 4.89 out of a possible five stars, and I took a great amount of pride in getting my passengers from point A to point B in a safe and timely fashion.

My first experience with Uber was surprisingly normal—well, almost normal. My goal was to start in the south suburbs where I lived and work my way downtown where the money was. Being a newbie at the time, I didn't have a full understanding of how the process worked, but I knew I could figure it out as I go.

The Dan Ryan Expressway had light traffic going northbound, and I headed to the Loop and didn't receive a fare until I reached 87th Street. Wow, my first fare, and I was excited and nervous at the same time. My phone chimed and flashed simultaneously as the Uber app indicator posted the address of a woman located on 83rd and Holland Road. What? The distance was only a half mile away, but I was unfamiliar with Holland Road. How could I not know where this street was being raised on the south side of Chicago? I had the option of accepting or rejecting the pickup, but I decided to accept it even though I didn't know exactly where to go.

I drove to Vincennes Avenue, where Simeon High School was, and the app kept redirecting me to the point of total confusion. My first fare was now sure to be a disaster, and the passenger was probably going to curse me out and give me a bad rating. I eventually figured out that Holland Road was where the new Walmart and Lowe's were located, and to my surprise, the lady was nice and understanding when I finally arrived at her pickup—a hair salon in the strip mall. She lived a few blocks away, and the conversation was pleasant. My first rating was five-star in spite of me getting lost. Thank God for that.

Finally, I was able to park in the Walgreens lot after it took me nearly ten minutes to drive a half-mile in rush hour traffic under hazardous conditions. I waited until the rain lessened in intensity before I went inside of the store to get my tea.

2

I had finished my burger and drunk one of my Arizona green teas while sitting in the Food-4-Less parking lot, which was still on the main Dolton strip on Sibley Boulevard. I had then logged into my Uber app and went online, and I waited for my first fare of the evening. My routine during the week was to work mid-morning to mid-evening Tuesday through Thursday (9:00 a.m. to 7:00 p.m.), and switch it up Friday and Saturday by working late afternoon to late night (5:00 p.m. to 3:00 a.m.). I would take Sunday and Monday off—Sunday was used as a day of rest, a time for Bible study and prayer, and quality time spent with my elderly parents, and I'd then use Monday to run errands or clean up my apartment, to name a couple of things. I had no social life or committed relationship to brag about—I also didn't hang out with any real friends, as time and space made strangers out of them—and I'd been single for almost six years after my three-year relationship with my girlfriend ended several months before I lost my job and hadn't found anyone special since then. However, my younger brother Jahlil, who lived out-of-state in Louisiana, was one of the few people who kept me sane and in contact with the outside world because we'd talk at least once a week.

The pay with Uber for me was good—I grossed on average $1250 to $1500 driving fifty hours per week, and fill-ups at the pump were roughly $125 to $150 per week as my 2010 Ford Fusion was very economical on gasoline. Another perk of driving for Uber was that I had write-offs that significantly lowered my taxes such as vehicle maintenance, mileage and auto insurance, for example.

My best earnings day to date was $812—due to the price surge on New Year's Eve—and my best week was $2507 during that same time frame. And my bad days were few—I once worked thirteen hours on a Monday and only earned a few bucks over one hundred dollars. Needless to say, I never drove on a Monday again after that.

The rain had started to pick up again, and my phone flashed and chimed minutes later. My pickup was at the Walgreens where I'd bought my tea earlier, and the guy's name was Charles. The rain was coming down at a steady pace, and it was getting more difficult to see in front of me. I pulled up inside the lot, and Charles, who appeared to be a high school kid, was waiting in front on the entrance trying not to get too wet. I parked in front of the entrance, pull my hazard lights on, and unlock my doors.

"How you doing, Charles?" I asked.

"Hi," he said, as he got himself situated in the back seat behind the passenger seat.

I preferred that people sat on the right side in the back, as opposed to sitting directly behind me, because I felt more comfortable if I could put my eyes on someone via my rear-view mirror. I also detested anyone sitting in my front seat unless it was absolutely necessary.

This kid had zero conversation—which was fine with me because I could flow either way—I could be a listening ear for a passenger and chime in every now and then, or we could ride in silence with the radio playing. The majority of my riders preferred to not talk and buried themselves in their phones, but a small percentage of them—maybe five or ten percent—did like to converse, which made for some interesting dialogue. I had picked up a pregnant young lady a week ago, and she was a sweet girl who basically gave me the entire spill of her baby-daddy issues with one of her children's fathers. The guy was a local rapper who had gotten another girl pregnant at the same time that my female passenger was, but the kicker was she wasn't upset about that situation because they didn't have a real commitment. She was upset because the baby daddy allowed the other woman to bring that drama to her house. That tidbit of information let me know that she was probably the side chick.

I started the trip on the app once Charles was buckled up, and his destination was a mile and a half west on Sibley Boulevard in Dolton. Well, technically his house was in Dolton, as the north side of the street was zoned as such, but the south side of the street was zoned Harvey. Traffic was still very heavy, and the rain only made matters worse. I was faced with a dilemma because visibility wasn't good, and I wasn't going to have an easy time trying to read Charles' address and slow down at the same time with all that traffic behind me. The address indicator on the app wasn't an exact science—it would usually say you've reached your destination about twenty to fifty yards before you were actually in front of a person's house. However, Charles realized that stopping in front of his house on a busy Sibley Boulevard in the rain wasn't a good option, so he graciously said, "You can make a right at the corner and park on the side. My house is two doors from the corner."

"Okay, thank you, Charles," I said.

I parked on the side of the street at the corner as he requested, and he proceeded to exit my car.

"Take care, Charles," I said.

"You, too," he said as he made a mad dash to his house.

I subsequently ended the trip and rated Charles a five and hoped he felt that his trip was a five under the circumstances. I currently didn't dwell on customer ratings the way I did in the beginning of driving for Uber back in 2014, because I learned that they'd vastly improved their rating system from years past. A bad rating could only count against you for navigation issues, conduct, safety issues, professionalism, tidiness, etc. Bad ratings for silly or superficial reasons like: *I didn't like his choice of music*, or *he parked one house down instead of parking in front of my house, and I had to walk to his car*. Drivers who got a string of complaints like that in the past were in danger of getting their app shut off, and that was very unfortunate and unfair.

The rain had started to subside somewhat, so I thought it was a good idea to venture out as opposed to staying in the neighborhood. I proceeded to head west toward Cicero Avenue and head north to Midway Airport. I knew I could always get a good fare there, but I got stopped by a freight train right at Ashland Avenue. Dream deferred, as they say.

3

I grew intensely tired of sitting in traffic waiting for the train to pass, so I busted a U-turn on Sibley and headed east to Vincennes Avenue. My goal was still to cop a fare at Midway Airport, but I was going to take an alternative route to get there. The time was 5:54 p.m., and before I could reach Vincennes, my phone lit up and chimed and led me to an address in Calumet City to pick up a woman named Mary. Traffic was still fairly congested but not total gridlock like it was thirty minutes ago, and I arrived at Mary's apartment complex in about fifteen minutes.

I then parked across the street, before I sent Mary a text that I was outside, and waited. Two minutes turned into five minutes, and five minutes turned into ten. I finally called her, and she answered on the fourth ring.

"Hello," she said, her speech slurred.

"Hi, it's Red, your Uber driver," I said, "and I'm parked outside your apartment. How soon are you coming out?"

"I'm sorry…give me a few more minutes."

"Okay."

"Damn, is she high?" I asked myself.

I looked at the clock on my dashboard that read 6:22 pm, and I sighed as I waited for Mary to come out. She was lucky that I was in a more patient mood than I was after dropping my first passenger, Charles, off, but I was beginning to get annoyed because she was messing up my money. Finally, after another ten minutes of waiting, she exited her building and headed toward my car, seemingly disoriented.

"Hi, Mary," I said.

"Hi," she said after she plopped in the back seat on the right side.

"Do you have enough room back there?"

"Yes."

I started the trip and proceeded to drive toward Interstate 94, which was a half-mile down the road. Mary's address was right off of 103rd and Halsted—not far from the field where Jackie Robinson West Little League played baseball. Everything seemed somewhat normal once I entered the expressway—well, almost normal. Every minute or so, I'd check on her to see if she was all right, because she was clearly intoxicated from her mannerisms and slurred speech.

Suddenly, Mary started coughing uncontrollably once we'd passed 111th Street and headed toward the Bishop Ford-Dan Ryan Expressway split. I thought initially that maybe she had motion sickness, so I slowed down ever so slightly, but to no avail, as her coughing intensified. I hope she doesn't throw up in my back seat, I thought. My first assumption of what may have been wrong with her was, and I was ashamed for thinking this, that she had HIV. She had the same cough Easy E had in the movie *Straight Outta Compton*, and if she didn't stop soon, I was going to call 911 because the last thing I needed was someone dying in my back seat.

Luckily and thankfully, her coughing and wheezing subsided once we exited the expressway at 99th and Halsted Street. We sat at the light at the intersection for a minute or so before I turned left on Halsted. Her house was about a mile away, and I couldn't wait to get rid of her.

I pulled up in Mary's driveway about five minutes later, and the most bizarre part of my night was about to happen. She was quiet most of the trip except for the coughing, but then she performed her Dr. Jekyll-Mr. Hyde routine right before my eyes.

"Thank you for getting me home safe, Red," she said as she dug into her purse. "You have to let me give you something."

"You're welcome," I said, "but you don't owe me anything."

"No, I really want to give you something. I have cash…"

"You don't have to give me cash…the app pays me for each fare."

Customers did tip me from time to time both from the app or with cash, but I wasn't about to take advantage of her because she was drunk. She had pulled out a wad of money from her purse, and an evil person with bad intentions would've taken everything she had.

"What about a fifth of Jose Cuervo?" she asked, trying to hand me the half-empty bottle. That explained why she was acting the way that she was.

"Nah, Mary, I'm good," I said.

"Are you sure that you don't want to have a nightcap with me? Because I'm a ride-or-die type of chick…"

If I had to rate Mary on a scale of one to ten, and my mind was totally not on doing anything sexually with her or any of my female customers, I'd give her fives all across the board. And I was being generous.

"I'm still on the clock, so I gotta get back to work."

"Oh, okay. You have a good night, handsome."

"Take care, Mary."

I watched her stagger inside of her house before I backed out her driveway. I definitely didn't want anything to happen to her on my watch. My only fear from that point on was getting a complaint for sexual harassment, even though nothing happened. However, her word against mine would probably result in my app being shut off.

4

I dodged a bullet in dealing with that Mary chick and her madness, so I decided to make my way north on Halsted to Interstate 57 and then merge onto the Dan Ryan Expressway and finally onward to the Loop area where I made my bread and butter. The plan was to grab as many fares as I could on a busy Friday night in a six-hour window and call it a night. The rain hadn't subsided, and Mary had drained some of my energy to the point of not wanting to deal with too many more fares, so I set my goal for the night at $200 instead of my customary $250. The northbound traffic on the expressway was flowing in spite of the weather, and I was at the 67th Street exit where the freeway divided into the express and local lanes in no time. However, my phone flashed and chimed, and next pickup was for Dave at an address right off 51st and State Street.

Thankfully, dusk hadn't set in yet, on this wet Friday evening in early May for my next fare—I parked and put my hazard lights on once I arrived at the destination a few minutes later. David was nowhere to be found, as I waited for him to show up. The address on my app led me to what appeared to be a storefront church, but there were no lights on or any sign of life there. My gut told me that I needed to get out of there pronto because it could've been a potential setup to rob or carjack me. I wasn't scared because God always had me, and besides, I had my Glock in the glove compartment on the passenger side. No worries, though, because I had a FOID card and CCL, so I wasn't riding dirty.

I decided not to drive off until the shot clock ran out—any given passenger was allotted a certain amount of time to show up before a driver could cancel a trip at his or her discretion and still get paid for waiting time. I didn't feel in danger waiting for Mary in Calumet City, but this trip felt totally different. Fortunately for me, Dave's time was finally up, so I canceled the fare and made $3.75 for my trouble.

I headed toward 47th and Cottage Grove Avenue once I went offline for a quick break, because the green tea that I consumed earlier had taken a toll on my bladder. There was a McDonald's on that corner, and the goal was to slip in and slip out once I'd used the bathroom. I had my spots throughout the city that I designated for bathroom usage—my favorite spot was the Jewel-Osco grocery store on Desplaines and Kinzie—which was a few blocks from my former employer.

I arrived at the McDonald's and quickly parked in the front of the restaurant before rushing to the bathroom. Once I handled my business, I exited the restaurant and hastened to my car, and it was then that I saw my ex-girlfriend, Marilyn, with her current beau in a shiny, black 2019 Mercedes-Benz. They were heading toward the drive-thru and didn't see me, and seeing her was like being suspended in time, because she'd clearly moved on and was seemingly happy with her present life, whereas for me it felt like the summer of 2013 all over again.

Our breakup wasn't nasty or anything close to it—she came home one day and said she wasn't in love with me anymore and packed her things and left. No warning or big blowup—or maybe the signs were right there in front of me, but I just didn't pay attention to them. I found out later on that she was seeing another guy behind my back for several months before she broke it off with me completely. I also realized that I wasn't really her type because this guy looked nothing like me—even though I considered myself to be a handsome dude, I was five foot ten and slim with the bare minimum of swag—no tattoos, no piercings, and no rhythm, and this guy looked like someone out of a GQ magazine—six foot two, light-skinned, and muscular. I knew deep down that I might've been dating out of my league because I earned an average salary of $40,000 annually at the time and drove a basic, 2010 Ford Fusion; and Marilyn was a dime-piece who was an independent woman with expensive tastes.

Even though Marilyn was the quote-unquote dream girl for me, I had a lot going for me as well. For starters, my appearance was always on point—my gear and kicks were fresh every day, and my fade and beard were tight. I also wooed Marilyn with my intellect and conversation—we met at the Black Women's Expo back in 2010 when I was selling my first self-published fiction novel, *Ulterior Motive*. She bought a copy from me, and I asked her out to dinner that same day. We ended up having a great time and were inseparable after that.

However, I'd had to put the dream on the back burner midway through my second novel a year later, because my first book hadn't been selling the way I'd envisioned it. My focus had shifted to recovering the thousands of dollars that I'd spent on marketing my book at various book fairs and with online advertising. My plan from that day forward had been to scale back and revamp my marketing strategy, but Marilyn had slowly withdrawn from me and eventually given up on our relationship as a result of me altering my business operation. I'd been blindsided by the breakup and lost twenty pounds from my already-slim frame that summer, and I'd found it extremely difficult to function at times. Marilyn had been my karma—I had paid the price for dogging out my previous girlfriend with the lies and the cheating. Thankfully, through many nights of prayer and repentance, I'd been able to turn my life around and get myself back on track. I then realized that putting my faith in the Lord was my only salvation, and I learned not to put too much faith in people for anything after that.

I took a moment to gather my thoughts before I went back online and left McDonald's parking lot. The new plan was to drive east on 47th Street all the way to the lakefront and head north toward the Loop on Lakeshore Drive. My Uber app had indicated another fare before I could even get past Cottage Grove Avenue, and my next pickup was in the Englewood neighborhood right off Garfield Boulevard and Union Avenue. I absolutely hated driving through Englewood, because if a murder or shooting took place in Chicago, it was a good chance that it happened there.

Shonda was waiting for me when I double-parked on the right side of the street and put my hazards on, and she was wearing what appeared to be pajama pants and a t-shirt. She was moderately tall for a woman—maybe five foot nine or ten, but I couldn't really tell if she was attractive or not because her appearance was disheveled like she had just gotten out of bed and walked out the house.

"Hi, Shonda," I said.

"Hi," she said, as she shut the rear passenger-side door behind her.

I started the trip, and luckily for me, the address was only about a half-mile away on 53rd and Princeton Avenue. I didn't want to spend anymore time in Englewood than I had to spend.

"Can we make another stop before you drop me off?" she asked.

"Where do you want to go?" I asked hesitantly.

"Oh, it's just around the block from my house on 52nd Place," she answered. "I'll only be a few minutes."

"Okay."

We arrived at 52nd Place off Princeton Avenue, and it was a dead-end street. Red flag. She then got out and walked inside the house. I looked at my clock, and it read 7:44 p.m. I didn't like the fact that my car was facing the dead-end corner of the block, so I made a U-turn so thar my car was facing Princeton Avenue instead. I checked my surroundings every so often and was prepared to jet if anything jumped off. I instantly sensed that I'd dropped her off at a trap house, because of the seedy characters circling the perimeter like vultures.

Shonda emerged from the house about five minutes later, so I unlocked the doors before she sat back in my car.

"Thank you, Red," she said.

"No problem," I said.

I didn't ask what her little pit stop was all about, and she didn't volunteer any information. The less I knew, the better off I was. I dropped her off around the block at her destination, and then I was off to my next adventure.

5

Getting a fare from Midway was still within reach because I was actually a little closer to the airport than the Loop, so I headed west on Garfield Boulevard en route to Cicero Avenue. There was a lot on 72nd and Cicero where all the Uber drivers congregated to wait for fares to become available. Sometimes the lot was empty and waiting time only five to fifteen minutes, but more often than not on a typical Friday night, the lot would probably be full. I would gauge whether or not it was worth the time to wait for a fare based on the number of cars ahead of me—I would wait if there were thirty cars or fewer in front of me in the queue. If there were more cars than that ahead of me, receiving a minimum fare of fifteen dollars, per se, from the airport after waiting more than thirty minutes was a waste of time.

Many of the people who I picked up from Midway were very interesting people from all walks of life—some were visiting Chicago while others were coming back from taking a trip somewhere. I met a nice couple from Kansas City once—they came to Chicago to experience all the attractions in the summertime, and I dropped them off at a restaurant they researched online on the north side of town. They also suggested that I try the barbecue if I ever visited their city.

I also picked up a nice young lady who came back to Chicago from visiting her family in San Diego. She was a student at the University of Chicago living in the Hyde Park area. She told me about some of the things tourists do in San Diego as well as how college life was for her in the big city. My favorite customer was actually a pickup going to Midway from downtown—a former minor league baseball player whose career was cut short due to an arm injury. He actually played with a current, prominent major league player in high school and alluded to the fact that this particular player used PEDs.

My phone went off after I passed Western Avenue, and my pickup was for a woman named Natalie. I arrived at her apartment in a few minutes and double-parked before turning my hazards on once again. She came out the house moments later and entered my vehicle, and I was taken aback by how attractive she was and how good she smelled. Or maybe my hormones were raging because I'd been single for a long time.

She was a beautiful Latina who was in her late teens or twenties, but who could tell these days? I said hello, and she spoke back before she put her seatbelt on and buried herself in her phone. Her destination was an apartment building a block away from the Dan Ryan Expressway on the north side of Garfield Boulevard.

We arrived there in less than ten minutes, and she had me drop her off in the alley next to the apartment. What guy would have her meet him in an alley with dusk starting to set in? Doesn't she have any respect for herself? I wondered if her family knew their precious daughter/niece/sister/cousin was probably meeting some lowlife degenerate in one of the worst neighborhoods in the city. I didn't have time to dwell on it because my app directed me to another pickup at the University of Chicago Hospital.

6

Desiree was the next passenger on deck for me to pick up at the main entrance of the University of Chicago Hospital off 58th and Maryland Avenue. She was standing out front when I arrived, with a pizza box in her hand, and she was dressed in hospital scrubs. I started the trip once she shut the door, and her address was in the heart of Englewood right off Garfield Boulevard and Carpenter Avenue. Damn.

"Hi, Desiree," I said.

"Hi, how are you doing?" she asked, as she fastened her seatbelt in the rear passenger side seat.

"I can't complain," I replied. "It doesn't do any good anyway."

"Ain't that the truth, but I guess it depends on who you ask."

"True. Man, that pizza smells good."

"You want a slice?"

"Nah, I'm good. I had a burger about an hour ago."

"Okay, let me know if you change your mind."

She was the first person that actually wanted to know how I was doing, and she sounded sincere when she asked. Even if she wasn't, it still felt good that she was courteous enough to inquire. She was also an attractive young lady who sounded intelligent whenever she spoke.

"So, are you a nurse?" I asked.

"No, I'm a phlebotomist," she replied.

"Oh—you draw blood from people. Do you like it?"

"I make decent money, but it's a means to an end, though."

"Are you in school?"

"Yeah, I take classes at DePaul in the morning and work here part-time."

"That's great. What's your major?"

"I just finished my second year in finance."

"That's what's up. Are you going to stay at the hospital when you graduate?"

"I don't know…maybe. Even though there's a broad range of opportunities there, I want to leave my options open."

"That's smart."

"So, is this your full-time job?"

"For the time being. Like you, I want to leave my options open."

"Do Uber drivers make good money?"

"It is what you make it. I do all right…some good days and some not-so-good days."

"I see. So, how long have you been driving for Uber?"

"A little over five years."

I always downplayed what I was earning from Uber—Desiree seemed like a nice girl, but I tried to never get too personal with my customers. I was asked this question quite often, but I didn't want people sizing me up by knowing exactly what I'd made every day. Uber was a great hustle for me because of the flexibility of dictating my own schedule, and Uber also allowed me to focus more on my writing than the rigid structure of corporate America allowed.

As for working the standard nine-to-five job, I didn't plan on going down that road ever again. I loved my freedom and cringed at the thought of dealing with office politics at any given firm.

"I thought about driving for Uber or Lyft because I have a cousin who does both, and she makes good money," she said. "However, I don't have reliable transportation, and I don't like driving that much."

"I understand," I said. "Uber isn't for everybody."

"What are most of the customers that you drive around like?"

"Well, to be honest, I wish more of them were like you…"

"Really?"

"All jokes aside, most of my customers are cool, but not as cool as you."

"That's nice to know, but I'm sure that you've had some bad experiences in the five years that you've been driving as well."

"Man, have I…and you don't know the half of it."

"What was the worst experience that you had?"

"The worst experience that I've had so far was with this R&B singing chick who was performing at this underground spot off

Ogden and Carroll Avenue on the near north side, and I'll never forget that her name was Jewel."

"I don't know of any clubs in that area...all I really have time for is work and school."

"I don't have much of a social life, either."

"I can totally relate to that."

I nodded and took a breath before saying, "I guess Jewel wasn't from Chicago, because I had a problem trying to find her location once I exited the Eisenhower Expressway at Canal Street. She had pinged it instead of keying in the exact address."

"How accurate is the map when someone pings their location?"

"It's not an exact science...sometimes it's spot-on and other times it'll send you a half-mile away from the actual location."

She nodded, and I continued, "So, I finally found her address, and it was an apartment complex right off I-290 near the Circle campus. I picked her up, and she was cool for most of the ride until we were a couple of blocks from the club."

"What did she do?"

"She started spazzing out because she was late for her performance, and I couldn't find the address because the block was dimly lit...and to make matters worse, she pinged the location instead putting in the exact address. She was very disrespectful and belligerent, and I finally told her to get out of my car after taking her abuse for about five minutes."

"Damn, you made her get out and walk?"

"Nope, because she quickly changed her tune after that. She pleaded with me and was extremely apologetic because she realized that she didn't know where the hell she was, and lucky, I found the club about minute later."

"Wow, that's crazy..."

"Yeah, it was, and needless to say, she was one of the few customers I rated one star."

I pulled up on Desiree's block and parked in front of her three-flat before putting my hazards on. There were also a group of guys standing around a few apartments down. I then turned around to get a good look at her before saying, "Thanks for the great conversation, and good luck with work and school."

"Likewise, Red," she said. "You should hurry up and get out of here, though. I'll be fine."

"Okay, I think you're probably right about that."

Desiree quickly got out the car and shut the door behind her, and I ended the trip before rating her five stars. I wasted no time driving off as I didn't want to test fate by hanging around too long. Those guys had probably robbed Uber drivers or anyone else on a regular basis, and sadly, I was no different from the next man.

Conversing with Desiree had dramatically lightened my mood, and I no longer had thoughts of ending my night earlier than I normally would've done on any given Friday. She was the type of woman I wished I'd met when I was in my mid-to-late twenties after I finished college—beautiful, smart, and classy—and she also seemed like the type of woman who liked who she liked and didn't care about a guy's rank in the social hierarchy, even though most of the women that I'd encountered in my lifetime had subscribed to it. I'd known women like her in college, but unfortunately for me, my circumstances hadn't allowed me to date one of them on a consistent basis. No money, no job, and no car at that time in my life had equaled no girlfriend.

My app indicator went off again before I could get too wrapped up in my thoughts about how guys ranked socially, and my pickup was off 63rd and Loomis Boulevard. Now here was where my night started to get very interesting.

7

Tameka lived around the block from the police station off 63rd and Loomis Avenue. Her block was a dead-end street, so I had to make a U-turn before I picked her up. She came out the house once the app indicated that I'd arrived, and she promptly sat in the back seat before I started the trip.

Boom, boom, boom, boom, boom! We had heard gunshots just a few yards away, but we didn't see anyone run out. I'd never heard shots in such close proximity to me, and it seemed as though the shooter was right behind us. I had quickly hit my brakes and ducked as soon as we heard the first shot.

"Are you all right?" I said, as I turned around to face her.

"Yes," she said, nodding her head.

I quickly sped off and didn't care about the police station that was around the corner. The nerve of someone firing a gun around a police station, I thought. I was at the Dan Ryan Expressway in no time and could hear sirens in the distance. I'd finally had time to focus on Tameka's address, and her destination was on 115th and Vincennes Avenue. Thank God that I had broken free of the vortex that kept pulling me back into the heart of Englewood.

Tameka was dead silent the entire ride and looked traumatized. She had that look that people have in war-torn countries—a confused expression, as if she had PTSD. It probably wasn't the first time she heard gunshots up close and personal, and unfortunately, it probably wouldn't be the last time.

I arrived at her house in about fifteen or twenty minutes and dropped her off. I looked at my clock after I ended the trip and rated Tameka a five, and it read a little after nine o'clock. I went offline once again and needed a break to clear my head. It isn't every day that gunfire erupts a few feet away from you, so taking a few minutes to process things was a necessity. There was a strip mall a half-mile away, off Interstate 57 and 119th Street, so I entered the lot and parked my car.

21

Every time a customer pissed me off or an uncomfortable situation arose, like the one that just took place, I'd reevaluate my reasons for driving. I had a long-term goal and wanted to stick to the plan but being in the direct line of fire of some idiots who had a beef with one another made me question whether or not driving for Uber was worth my time. I had an initial one-hundred-thousand-dollar IRA that I'd rolled over from my previous job, and I paid into it monthly with a portion of my Uber earnings while collecting interest, and my social security monthly payments would be about fifteen hundred dollars and change per month once I turned sixty-two. Add my growing monthly book royalties to the mix, and I'd have a comfortable income once I retired. However, if I kept having to deal with stressful and dangerous encounters with people while driving for Uber, my only option would be to quit.

I glanced at my phone and saw that I've only made $54.27 in almost four hours on the road. I then sighed and shut my eyes for a few minutes. I had the thought of packing it in and going home, but I decided to tough it out instead. I then opened my eyes and stared at a hollow shell of a once-thriving Target store that was now permanently closed.

The rain began to get heavy again, and I went back online and resumed driving. My phone went off a few minutes later, and my pickup was for Amber in the suburb of Harvey.

8

I arrived at Amber's house in about ten minutes as Interstate 57 was only a block away from the strip mall where I had parked for a few minutes to clear my head. The rain was still falling at a steady pace, and she came out moments later with a box of party favors that she placed on her front porch. I got out the car and assisted her.

"Hi, Amber," I said, as I placed her stuff in the back seat on the drivers side.

"Hi, Red," she said. "I have a few more items to bring out."

"Okay."

Amber returned a minute or so later with some balloons and more party decorations that we placed in the back seat, and she sat in the front passenger side seat when we were done. She was a slim and pretty, blond-haired Caucasian woman who was dressed in a tight-fitted, red-and-black-striped dress that came a couple of inches above the knee. She also had on a thin, black leather jacket and six-inch stilettos that matched her outfit perfectly. I started the trip and drove off in the direction of Interstate 294, which was about a mile and a half away from her house. Her destination was an address in the township of Bridgeview.

"Thank you so much," she said.

"You're very welcome," I said. "What's the occasion?"

"We're throwing a birthday party for my boss at work."

"That's nice. Where do you work?"

"I dance at Polekatz."

"Oh, yeah, I've seen the billboard for that club. Do you like it?"

"Yeah, I make good money there, and my boss is a nice guy. I've been there for a little over a year."

"That's cool. I've been driving for Uber for five years."

"That's great. How do you like driving for Uber?"

"It's okay...I have good days and bad days just like any other job."

"I totally understand."

I paused briefly before asking, "How long have you lived in Harvey?"

"I just bought my house about a month ago," she answered.

"Congratulations."

"Thank you."

"I've been living in Calumet City since 2006. I stay in the Sandridge Apartments."

"I thought about living there once, but I decided that it would be better to buy a house."

"I live alone, so I don't need that much space. A two-bedroom apartment is a perfect fit for me."

"How much do you pay in rent?"

"I pay $1100 per month."

"Damn, that's almost as much as I pay for my mortgage."

"Yeah, it all balances out though…when something breaks, it's the landlord's job to fix it. I also don't have to worry about paying high taxes every six months."

"True."

I entered the expressway a few minutes later and paid the toll electronically via the I-Pass—an absolute must if you were a driver, because most tolls were half-priced with a transponder located on the windshield.

Amber took a breath before asking me, "Do you have anyone special in your life?"

"I'm afraid not," I answered. "I did once, but things didn't work out."

"What happened?"

"We grew apart because we didn't want the same things out of life."

"I'm sorry to hear that."

"It's okay…everything happens for a reason. I guess it just wasn't meant to be, you know."

"Yeah, I know."

"What about you?"

"My boyfriend and I are solid. We plan on getting married soon."

"That's good. If you don't mind me asking, how does he feel about you dancing?"

"That's a fair question. He didn't like it at first…he's still not totally on board with it, but he trusts me. I started doing it to save money for my house, and now I've gotten used to making this kind of money."

"I get it."

"How about you? Does Uber pay you well?"

I normally didn't answer that question directly, but since Amber was so honest with me about her situation, I reciprocated the gesture.

"I'm not going to lie," I said, "I make good money doing this."

"How much is good money?"

"A good week for me is about fifteen hundred on average, and my best week was a little over twenty-five hundred dollars one year during the Christmas and New Year's holidays."

"Good for you, Red. A good night for me would be a grand…my best night was a little over two, but I ended up owing a hundred dollars once to cover my house fee on my worst night ever."

"How many nights do you work?"

"Three or four, usually. I'm about to finish school and become a nurse."

"What school do you attend?"

"I'm in the nursing program at South Suburban College, and I'll receive my associate degree next month."

"Congratulations, again."

"Thank you."

"So, what are your immediate plans after graduation?"

"I have enough money saved to quit dancing so that I can start looking for a job in my field."

"That's great."

We were at the club before we knew it, and I double-parked at the entrance and helped Amber get her stuff from the back seat. One of her coworkers was waiting for us to pull up, and I handed her the box of party favors, as there was a slight drizzle falling.

"Thank you so much, Red," Amber said, giving me a hug and a kiss on the cheek. "Take care."

"You, too," I said. "Good luck with your career."

"Thanks."

I quickly got back in the car and ended the trip before rating Amber five stars. She was, by far, one of the most pleasant passengers I ever had. I then made a U-turn and exited the lot, as the club was positioned a half-block off the main street down a dark and narrow road. My earnings were now over seventy-five dollars, and I was starting to feel a little better about the night in general.

My phone went off again before I could get too comfortable, and it was a pickup in Palos Hills for a man named Bart. This trip would ultimately prove to be the defining moment in my driving career for Uber—a journey that would ultimately test my faith as a Christian.

9

Your enemy is the gateway to your future.
—Dr. Michael Murdock

Palos Hills was only a few minutes from the club, and I put my hazard lights on after I parked on this quiet suburban block. I had envisioned my rider to be a young Caucasian male because Palos Hills was a predominantly white suburb. However, the person who emerged from the house was a slim black guy who was about five foot ten or eleven with a hoodie, a baseball cap, and sagging, skinny-legged jeans on. This kid couldn't have been no more than twenty-one years old, but he had a dark aura that made me slightly uncomfortable at first. He was talking on his cell phone when he entered my car and sat in the back seat on the passenger side.

"What's up?" I asked.

He nodded at me and continued his phone conversation, and I started the trip before driving off. His destination was to an address off 83rd and Loomis, so the app directed me to 95th and Harlem Avenue, and then eastbound on 95th Street.

Bart was very aggressive toward whomever he was arguing with on the phone, and he let off some choice expletives to get his point across. I wasn't trying to hear his conversation and didn't exactly know what had ticked him off, and I didn't care. My mission was to drop Bart (probably not his real name) off to his destination and keep it moving. Thankfully, he finally ended his call after a couple of minutes. He had an arrogance about him that was revealed in his diatribe, and I had an instant dislike for him even though I kept it professional and didn't show it. My first impression of him was that he was a degenerate who was probably waist-deep in some form of criminal activity, and I was spot-on in my assessment of him.

"Do you have bluetooth in your car?" he asked.

"No, but I have an aux cord," I answered, as I reached in my glove compartment behind the gear shift panel—my Glock was in the glove compartment on the passenger side, and I didn't want to reveal that I had one. The cord wasn't there, so I knew it had to be in the compartment where my gun was. Sure enough, the cord was coiled underneath it.

"Here you go," I said after I reached inside the glove compartment and quickly and carefully pulled the aux cord out.

He plugged it inside his phone, and I set my radio to auxiliary mode after I plugged my end on the cord in the auxiliary outlet in the compartment behind the gear shift panel. He picked some track that had more curse words in it than a classic NWA rap song, and I tried my best to hide my disgust for his playlist.

"Can you turn it up?" he asked.

"Okay," I said, taking a deep breath before I adjusted the volume on my steering wheel.

The blasphemous lyrics blared through the speakers, and the bass rattled the frame of the car. Now don't get me wrong—I didn't mind that my passengers listened to the radio or their own personal playlists loudly, because I was very liberal in that regard, and I allowed all of the young adults who'd had the pleasure of sitting in my back seat do this. Also, I wasn't always this prudish, either, but at forty-five years of age, I'd lost the desire to listen to this type of music once I became a born-again Christian. I was a rap-head in my younger days and could recite the lyrics of a Nas, Ice Cube, or Tupac cut with the best of them, but when my soul was cleansed with the Holy Spirit, most of my sinful desires were washed away. However, I still enjoyed listening to the classics like Marvin Gaye, James Brown, or Sade, for example, and I still like to listen to house music.

It also dawned on me that this underground rap song might have been his because he looked like one of those no-talent mumble-rappers in his appearance. I tried to give him the benefit of the doubt and didn't want to label him as a criminal just yet.

"Is that you?" I asked.

"Nah, man," he answered after he chuckled.

"Oh, okay."

I looked at him from my rear-view mirror, and he focused his complete attention on his phone. He looked up a few seconds later and said, "You keep a clean car, Uber."

"Thanks, man. I appreciate it," I said.

"What year is your Ford Fusion?"

"It's a 2010."

"I had a car, but I ended up selling it."

"Why did you sell it?"

"I got tired of the police harassing me all the time."

"Yeah, they profile people in this area a lot."

The police wouldn't be harassing you all the time unless you were into shady stuff, I thought. Police did random checks on anyone's license plates, so this was nothing new. I figured out that Bart got rid of his car in order to stay below the radar, and I also figured out that he probably used Uber drivers as mules to assist him in whatever shady activity he was involved in. He was probably trying to size me up to see if I'd be a good fit to his criminal enterprise.

"I had a guy drive me around so that I could handle my business," he said, "but he had to quit about a month ago."

"Did he drive for Uber?" I asked.

"Yeah, he would coordinate his schedule around mine so that he could only drive for me."

"Why did he quit?"

"His wife didn't want him driving for me anymore because I had him out too late, I guess."

"I see."

He paused for a moment and then he asked, "What's your schedule like?"

"I have a set schedule working Monday through Friday in the downtown area," I lied, "and I only drive for Uber part-time on the weekends."

"Okay," he said.

There was no way in hell that I would drive for this guy. The nerve of him, I thought. My phone chimed, and I noticed that he changed the address as I was approaching my turn on Ashland Avenue.

"What's up?" I asked. "Do you want me to keep straight?"

"Yeah…change of plans."

"Okay."

I had seen that the new address was off of 97th and Lowe Avenue. I proceeded to stay on 95th Street as we passed Ashland Avenue instead of making a left turn. My adventure was about to become even more disturbing.

10

I pulled up in front of a house on 97th and Lowe, and we waited. Bart's phone was steadily chiming, and he was totally engrossed in texting whoever the person or persons were blowing up his phone. I turned the radio back on because he hadn't picked another song from his raunchy playlist yet. A few minutes later, his partner in crime came out the house and walked toward the car. I unlocked the car, and he sat in the back seat next to Bart.

"What's up, my man?" I asked firmly.

He paused for a split second and said, "Hello."

"Hello?" Bart asked before he laughed. "Man, you sound like a goofy."

His flunky laughed it off and didn't say anything. My guess was he was the guy Bart cursed out earlier. This dude looked like the typical, dread-headed young man from Chicago and didn't stand out to me in any kind of way whatsoever. He appeared to be quiet and unassuming, so I didn't pay him any mind at first.

Bart then programmed another address in the app, and it was to an address in the suburb of Country Club Hills. I then headed toward Interstate 57 and merged onto the southbound lanes.

Bart and his right-hand man were conversing in a low volume, so I was able to tune them out and focus on the road. We arrived at the Martec International warehouse about fifteen or twenty minutes later, and I parked in the lot behind the entrance. Bart's right-hand man got out the car, and Bart and I waited. Five minutes turned into ten, and ten minutes turned into twenty. I looked at the clock, and it was a few minutes after eleven. Bart continued to receive texts on his phone and was busy answering them, and I was growing more and more impatient and angry because Bart wasn't being forthright about what they were actually doing there. I wasn't about to be a mule for this punk and risk going to jail, so I confronted him.

"Hey, bruh," I said. "What the hell is going on?"

"What?" he asked tersely.

"I didn't stutter. Why are we waiting here? I don't have time to be wasting with y'all all night…"

"Not your concern, Uber."

"Dude, who the hell do you think you're talking to? I'll be damned if I'm gonna get mixed up in your BS."

"Why are you trippin', man? You get paid regardless if we're moving or not, so chill."

"For your information, I get paid by the mile and by the time, so I'm losing money fooling around with you and your man right now."

"Look, my man will be out in a few minutes…"

"Dude, I don't know what y'all are into, and I don't wanna know. I'm ending this trip right now, and you need to get out of my car…"

"Not so fast, Uber. You know that I saw your *whistle* in your glove compartment, don't you?"

"Yeah, so what?"

"So, what do you think Uber would do if they knew about it?"

"Are you threatening me? Because I could get you shut down too, Bart, or is Bart even your real name?"

He laughed and said, "Relax, man, I'm not gonna bust your balls 'cause I ain't a snitch. I just need you to hang with us for a few hours, and then we'll be outta your life forever. Do we have an understanding, dawg?"

I paused briefly before answering, "Yeah, we have an understanding…but I'm a ghost after one o'clock."

"All right."

Bart's homeboy finally came back to the car, and another one of their cohorts accompanied him. This guy was a runt—maybe five foot six or seven and thin, and he was dressed almost exactly like Bart. I also noticed that Bart's right-hand man had a little size on him standing about six feet and probably weighing about two hundred pounds. If something had popped off, he'd be the one I'd be most concerned about.

Flunky number two sat in the front seat next to me while the other one sat back in his seat next to Bart. Bart then programmed another address into the app, and we were off to a nearby address in the township of Markham near the municipal courthouse.

"What's up?" I asked the new guy.

"I'm good," he answered.

My seatbelt indicator started chiming a half-mile from the warehouse, and the young man next to me didn't have his seatbelt on.

"Seatbelt, my man," I said. "I wouldn't want anything to happen to you if some idiot happened to plow into me."

"My bad," he said, as he fastened his seatbelt.

I wondered what those two knuckleheads were doing at the warehouse—the new guy wasn't dressed in any type of security uniform, and they were in the warehouse together for at least forty-five minutes after we pulled up. I told Bart that I didn't want to know what they were into, and I meant it for my own protection. However, I couldn't help but wonder if there was a female security guard at that warehouse who may have paid them for sex—I wasn't always saved, and the thought did cross my mind.

Bart's right-hand turned his attention away from Bart and asked me out the blue, "How long have you been driving, Uber?"

I looked at both of them from my rear-view mirror, and Bart had a devilish grin on his face. I guess they were trying to intimate me or something to that effect because this guy was as quiet as a church mouse prior to the meeting at the warehouse.

"Not long," I lied again. "It's just a way for me to make some extra money."

"I feel you," he said. "You look familiar…where did you go to high school?"

"I went to Kenwood Academy," I answered.

"Oh, okay," he said. "I thought you went to Harlan."

"I'm a little older than you guys, so I guess I have a double somewhere out here," I said.

"How old are you?" Bart asked.

"I'm forty-five," I answered.

"Yeah?" Bart asked. "You don't look forty-five."

"I'm afraid I am," I said.

"Do you know something about card cracking?" his right-hand man asked.

"Nah, I can't say that I do," I answered. "Why?"

"Because I'm looking for somebody to crack this card that I got," he answered. "Do you know somebody who works at a bank?"

"I'm afraid not, my man," I answered.

That explained why this crew had money to burn by having Uber drivers chauffeur them around town all damn night with fake accounts. These guys were rotten to the core.

"You're rich, aren't you?" the right-hand man asked.

"Nope, I'm far from that," I answered.

"I don't believe you," he said. "You got the fresh gear on, and your car is dope, Uber."

"I appreciate the compliment," I said, "but I gotta hustle to make ends meet just like everybody else."

My car did look good on the outside with rims, Pirelli tires, and a fresh paint job, but I'd almost driven it to the moon and back because my odometer read a little over 175,000 miles. A new car was definitely in my plans for the near future.

I missed my exit at 159th Street as a semi that was moving very slowly to my right way and prevented me from getting over to the exit in time. I sighed before saying, "Sorry I missed the exit, Bart."

"Now you're costing me money, Uber, but don't worry about it," he said. "Just keep straight."

"All right," I said.

Bart and his right-hand man turned their attention away from me and started roasting the new guy who sat quietly in the passenger seat. He struck me as a guy who didn't really fit in and was trying to prove himself, and they had no respect for him whatsoever. Bart programmed the new address in the app to an address in the Alsip area off 119th and Pulaski Road. The saga continued as I traveled northbound on I-57.

11

I was slowly starting to put the pieces of the puzzle together as far as what these future residents of Cook County jail were ever-so-entrenched in. We were on our way to pick up the entertainment for the night as I cruised west down 119th Street amidst the steady rainfall that had picked up once again. Bart's phone kept chiming as the other two guys were laughing and joking with each other, and Bart had resumed with his playlist from hell. I continued to focus on the road and had nothing to say.

The sexual underworld is a very lucrative industry to be in, as my previous passenger Amber had alluded to with how much cash she made on any given night. Bart had somehow managed to carve himself a niche in this murky environment, and the fact that his phone had been sounding off the entire time he'd been in my car suggested that he was highly skilled in recruiting young women who were ready and willing to serve him in whatever capacity he needed them in. I looked at my rear-view mirror and studied Bart briefly while he was totally engrossed in his phone. Nothing really stood out about him, except for the fact that he sort of resembled the actor Columbus Short. However, this young man undeniably had charisma, a trait that was essential in this business.

I was no stranger to this dark and nebulous world—I've been to enough bachelor parties, birthday celebrations, and nightclubs that featured exotic dancers to make a qualified assessment as to what was really going on with this crew. I knew how these young women got down, and I knew that it didn't take a whole lot of experience to make a ridiculous amount of money stripping. I'd witnessed a young woman work a room and leave with over a thousand dollars for thirty minutes of work once, back in the day.

A good friend of mine, who grew up with me, had turned thirty some years ago, and his mother had thrown him a birthday party. Midway through the party, his mother had surprised us all by hiring an exotic dancer for the entertainment that evening. The dancer was accompanied by a bodyguard, and all of us were entranced by how beautiful this chick was. To get a good idea of how sexy this stripper looked, she was almost a dead ringer for the actress Melyssa Ford. Needless to say, she was paid five hundred dollars up front, and we made it rain for thirty minutes straight before she walked away with an additional windfall of cash.

Some years later, another friend of mine was about to get married, and we all had thrown him a bachelor party at a motel in the south suburbs. We had booked a suite, bought food and drinks, and waited for the dancers to show up. There was also a young lady there who was so beautiful and sexy that some of us thought she was part of the entertainment. We would later find out that she was great friends with the groom-to-be's nephew.

The girls finally showed up an hour or so later, because they had done a previous party before coming to our hotel suite. They came cheap at two hundred fifty dollars, because they were also friends of the groom-to-be's nephew. A couple subsequently worked the room doing lap dances while another one was turning tricks in the second room of the suite. I inconspicuously managed to dip out of there before things had gotten too crazy.

My last experience before I got saved was at a strip club in the south suburbs that another one of my soon-to-married friends wanted to go after his bachelor party was over. There were four of us in total who ended up going to the club, and it was a packed house. We then ended up getting a table before we ordered some drinks. Moments later, this gorgeous young woman named Melinda walked up to our table and introduced herself. She wasn't voluptuous like the typical stripper—she was built more like a fashion model, with long and shapely legs and a slim frame, but there was something very alluring about her. Her captivating smile, her sexy white dress which hugged every curve of her body, and the scent of her Egyptian Musk body oil had the four of us mesmerized.

This young woman was in essence a true alpha female—a woman who totally embraced her femininity and who could tap into the reptilian part of any man's brain and seduce him into giving her anything she wanted without coercion or aggression. She worked the four of us and walked away with forty dollars or more in lap dances from each one of us in less than an hour. In fact, I'd be willing to bet my night's earnings that she probably majored in psychology in college, because she knew exactly how to stroke a man's ego to the point that she would literally have men fighting each other for a chance to eat out of the palm of her hand. Many red-pill dudes who claimed to be immune to the tomfoolery of the average woman would change their tunes quickly if they encountered someone like Melinda.

I looked at my clock that read 12:03 a.m. and sighed. The apartment complex where the girl or girls lived was a block away, so I parked in front of the apartment a couple of minutes later and waited. Five minutes had passed, and Bart was steadily texting whomever. Damn, these youngsters don't believe in talking to each other on the phone, I thought.

"Come on, Uber, let's blow this joint," Bart said, after we waited an additional five minutes.

"Okay," I said as I made a U-turn and headed back to Pulaski Road.

"Yo, can we go to that McDonald's on the corner?" his right-hand man asked.

"Sure, no problem," I answered.

This particular McDonald's was a twenty-four-hour spot, so I asked, "Y'all going inside or the drive-thru?"

"Nah, I wanna go inside," Bart answered.

"Me, too," his right-hand man said.

"What about you, fam?" Bart asked his third wheel.

"Nah, fam, I'm gonna chill," he answered.

"Okay," Bart said.

"You want something to eat, Uber?" the right-hand man asked.

"Nah, I'm cool, bro," I said. "Thanks for asking."

"Okay," he said.

Bart and his homeboy got out the car and went inside of McDonald's to order their food. I studied them as they approached the front counter and realized the real reason why Bart wanted to go inside as opposed to going through the drive thru. There were two scantily clad young women in line ahead of them, and if I were a betting man, Bart was telling them how they could make some quick cash stripping at a house party with a bunch of thirsty guys ready and willing to tip them. I then glanced at their partner-in-crime sitting next to me and asked, "How come you didn't go inside with your boys?"

"I didn't want nothing to eat," he answered.

He seemed unsure of himself and was probably struggling internally with his reasons for being there in the first place. I felt like it was possible to reach this kid—maybe drop a jewel on him before his friends got back to the car. Everyone was redeemable until they took their last breath, and God only knew a person's ending. However, his other two cohorts had totally embraced the dark side, and my preaching to them would've undoubtedly fallen on deaf ears.

"Why do you hang out with them?" I asked.

"I don't know," he answered. "Why do you ask?"

"I don't want to sound harsh, but I'm gonna give it to you straight, young buck. Those guys don't respect you, and it's only a matter of time before they end up in the county jail. You don't have to go down with them."

"I know, man, and I hear what you're saying...but I don't have nothing else going on in my life right now."

"Anything is better than going to jail, and nothing is worth your freedom, man. Just something to think about."

"Okay."

"Do you know God?"

"Huh? Nah, man, I ain't going to no church."

"You don't need church to find God. All you have to do is pray to God with a pure heart, repent of all your sins, and ask Him for forgiveness."

"Just like that, huh?"

"Yeah, just like that. I'm telling you from personal experience that if you take two steps toward God, He'll take ten steps toward you. I was in the world once...I used to drink, get high, and sleep with as many women as I could. Hell, I even sold weed while I was in college, to get by and pay my rent."

"You were a d-boy, Uber?"

"Yeah, I was in the game for a couple of years back in the day."

"You ever get busted?"

"Nah, I wasn't moving enough weight to get busted—my clientele was mostly college students, and I got out the game before I got on the cops' radar."

"What made you turn your life around?"

"I was tired of feeling empty inside, you know. I was thirty-nine years old at the time, and all my friends were getting married, raising their children, and living well. I wasn't being blessed because I was living a sinful life, and God showed me in a dream I had that if I continued down the path I was headed, I would go straight to Hell when I died."

"So, it was at that point that you turned your life over to God?"

"Yes, it was six years ago, and it was the best decision that I ever made. God has blessed me more than I could ever imagine, and I'm free for the first time in my life."

"What do you mean by being free?"

"I'm my own boss, young buck. I could quit driving for Uber tonight if I wanted to...between me and you. I do it because I want to, not because I have to."

The young cohort was in deep though after my last affirmation. Finally, the other two came back to the car with their food. I looked at my clock, and it read 12:26 a.m.

"Damn, I almost had them," Bart said. "We need to scoop up those chicks in Marynook, though."

"Yeah, let's go get 'em," his right-hand man suggested.

"Can you hang out with us a little longer, Uber?" Bart asked.

"How long is it going to take?" I asked. "It's almost one o'clock, and I've got a busy day tomorrow."

"Come on, man," Bart said, "you can at least hang with us until we scoop these girls over in Marynook. I'll type in the address now."

"Yeah, Uber, it won't take too much longer, I promise," his right-hand man said.

"All right, but after that, I'm gone," I said.

Bart keyed the address in the app, and we were off to a house off

87th and Kenwood. So much for ending my night early, I thought.

12

We arrived at the next destination in about fifteen minutes, and I parked outside the house and waited after the crew got out and walked up to the front porch of the house. Bart rang the doorbell, and the three of them went inside once a young lady answered the door. Good. They didn't flake on them like the other women had done in Alsip—I was ready for this night to end, and if these girls had decided to renege on their agreement with these degenerates, I would have left them stranded right where they were.

Bart's right-hand man came back outside about five minutes later and walked toward the car. I rolled down the passenger side window and asked, "What's going on in there?"

"The girls will be ready in a few minutes," he answered.

"How many of them are there? I technically only have room for one more passenger."

"It's three of them altogether. One can sit in the middle and the other two can sit on our laps."

"Okay, but if I get stopped, y'all are paying the ticket."

He laughed and asked, "Can you do me a favor?"

"What is it?"

He reached in his pocket and pulled out three wrinkly dollars and asked, "Can you pick up a pack of condoms for me?"

"All right, but you're pushing, man," I said.

"You're not gonna leave us, are you?"

"Nah, I'll be outside when y'all come out."

"Okay, you make sure you don't leave us, Uber," he said, before he ran back into the house.

I shook my head and drove to the gas station that was right on the corner. Damn, this dude was so thirsty. I realized at this point that he was merely a hanger-on and not really a partner-in-crime—someone who was merely there to help recruit and sleep with the entertainment—a flunky if you will. He was a likable guy nonetheless, but he reminded me of Jerome from the R&B group The Time because he went along with whatever Bart said or did.

I parked in front of one of the gas pumps and went inside. I then asked the clerk for a three-pack of condoms that cost three dollars and change, but luckily, I had some cash on me as homeboy was a little short. The crew was still inside when I parked back in front of the house, so I waited once more. Ten additional minutes passed by before the six of them came outside. The girls looked underage as they approached the car, and they might've been eighteen years old at best. One girl sat in the middle of Bart and his sidekick, and the other two sat on each of their laps while young buck sat back in the front.

"Hello, young ladies," I said.

"Hello," they all said in unison.

"Do you know where the little strip mall is on 95th Street in between Stony and Cottage Grove, Uber?" Bart asked.

"Yeah, it's on 95th and Woodlawn," I answered.

"Go there, and I'll type in the next address after that," Bart instructed.

"Okay," I said.

I was right at 87th and Cottage Grove Avenue when Bart made the suggestion, so I made a left turn and headed south on Cottage Grove Avenue. I then made another left turn on 95th Street and headed east until we got to the strip mall on Woodlawn Avenue. I parked in one of the spaces and waited.

I tuned out the mindless banter being exchanged between these young men and women and reflected on my night in general up to that point. Being shot at and propositioned by a drunk woman didn't seem so bad after hanging out with this band of misfits. I was also starting to get a migraine that I couldn't seem to shake off.

It wasn't hard to figure out why Bart had to pick his entertainment up instead of meeting up with them at the spot because these girls were, in fact, underage. This made it much easier for Bart to manipulate and exploit them, but the flip side of the coin was that Bart wasn't entirely at fault here because none of those girls was innocent. They were also ready and willing to give up her most prized possession without hesitation.

Moments later, a brown, beat-up-looking Chevy had pulled up and parked on Woodlawn Avenue, and Bart got out to meet him. My guess was that Bart bought some weed and Molly for the private party taking place a little later on. He then came back to the car couple of minutes later, and we were off. The expressway was a half-mile away, and Bart keyed in the next address—a residence in Country Club Hills. I felt like we were going in circles at this point, but I was also relieved somewhat because my night was coming to an end soon.

One of the young ladies decided that she wanted to break away from their group conversation and talk to me for a minute. I looked out my rear-view mirror at Bart, and he didn't appear to be too thrilled about it.

"How do you like driving for Uber?" she asked.

"It's okay," I answered.

"Have you been driving for a long time?"

"Nah, not long."

"You have a very nice car…you have it looking so clean."

"Thank you, sweetheart."

"I have a brother that makes good money driving for Uber…"

"Yeah, you have your good days and bad days…you get out of it what you put into it."

"Um hum."

She asked me a few more questions, but I keep the conversation to a bare minimum. We were approaching the 127th Street exit, and Bart and his crony sitting beside me couldn't decide on whether or not they should go to the Country Club Hills address. They probably realized that it was too late to do more than one private party and had to decide which one was the most logical and lucrative to do.

"Get off at 147th Street, Uber," Bart said. "We're going back to my spot."

"Okay," I said.

He put his address in the app, and I suddenly had a burst of energy because I was excited about finally getting rid of Bart and his subordinates. I hit I-294, which was a few blocks away from I-57 like a bat out of hell and was back in Palos Hills in no time. We pulled up in front of Bart's house, and there were a few guys hanging out front, and more guys inside as the front door was wide open. Bart and his right-hand man got out the back, and the girls followed suit. The young buck was the only one who said goodbye, and I shook his hand and said, "Remember what I told you. You always have a chance to turn things around while you're still living...don't let that chance slip away."

He nodded and said, "Okay."

"Take care."

"Take care, big homie."

The young buck got out of the car, and I belted out a sigh of relief as I ended the trip and rated Bart one star before I drove off. I cracked open my second can of Arizona green tea and gulped it down my throat, after I went offline for the last time and completely logged off my app. My total earnings for the night were unknown at the time because the app was still in the process of calculating the numbers.

I looked at the time, and it was a few minutes after two o'clock. Interstate 294 was a few blocks away as I sat at a traffic light.

"Damn, I can't believe I spent four hours with these clowns," I said to myself.

The light finally turned green after a minute of waiting, and I was on the expressway going southbound soon afterwards. I was mentally and spiritually drained, and I felt like I just went twelve rounds fighting for the heavyweight boxing title of the world. My only thought at the time was getting to my bed as quickly as possible.

13

It was a little after two thirty in the morning when I turned my key in the lock and opened the door of my apartment, and I wearily stepped inside and tossed my keys on the living room table. I then sighed and plopped down on the sofa. My headache had subsided, thankfully, so I grabbed the remote and turned on the television to see if I could catch some sports highlights. Playoff basketball was in full bloom, but I wasn't too interested in it because the Bulls didn't make it.

I was totally disgusted with myself for compromising my morals and allowing Bart to dictate my night. I was a willing participant in this debauchery and deserved to have my Uber app shut down. I had a choice—I had free will—but I decided to make a deal with the devil instead. I could've stood my ground and kicked Bart out of my car, but I allowed him to blackmail me by holding the gun in the glove compartment over my head. I chose my livelihood over doing the right thing, and because of this, I prayed to God for forgiveness half of the ride home.

Bart could still report me and get my app shut down permanently, and besides, I'm almost certain that Bart wasn't his real name and certain that his Uber account was fake. So, it would make no difference if I reported him—he'd just open up another fake account because Uber didn't do background checks on their customers.

My stomach was growling as I realized that I hadn't eaten since the early evening of the previous day, but I didn't want to eat anything heavy or greasy because I was also tired and would be asleep soon. I remembered that I had some grapes and some pasta salad in the fridge, so I made this my late-night snack. I had finally found something on television worth watching before I went to the kitchen to make my plate. One of my favorite Westerns was on— *The Quick and the Dead* staring Sharon Stone, Russell Crow, and Gene Hackman.

I usually recapped my day each time that I had driven for Uber—reflecting on the customers that had given me great conversation and customers that I wanted to kick out my car like Bart. An average day for me was picking up anywhere between twenty-five and forty customers as the Uber pool allowed me to garner fares in clusters, but surprisingly, I didn't get any Uber pools on this particular night. Most of the customers who rode in my back seat didn't leave a lasting impression, and that was fine with me because I also enjoyed the silence as well as the good dialogue with passengers.

I plucked a couple of grapes off the vine and ate them, and then I logged on to the Uber app to see how much I earned for the night. I had eight fares and one cancellation, for a total of $246.22—almost four dollars short of my nightly goal. Damn. I also saw that I only earned $131 slumming with Bart and his cronies for four hours straight—a far cry from the $700 dollars Bart had boasted that his previous driver had earned driving him around one night. I had earned $115 and a $40 tip on one fare last summer for two hours of work after I took two couples back to Bloomington, Illinois from downtown Chicago. The four of them were in town for a Cubs-Cardinals divisional rivalry, as they were Cardinal fans. I then looked at the breakdown of each fare and noticed that Amber tipped me forty dollars in the app. Great. She now definitely ranked in the top five of my all-time favorite customers with her kind gesture. My rating didn't change and was still 4.89—with well over twenty thousand trips under my belt, my Uber rating was etched in stone.

Once again, I questioned myself why I still continued to drive for Uber. I put myself in harm's way when I picked up Tameka in the heart of Englewood, and I probably broke several laws after I picked up Bart. Customers like Amber and Desiree made driving worthwhile, but the five percent of rotten apples that I've driven around over the years made me want to quit. I had saved enough money to close up shop over the course of five years of driving, and I had a healthy stream of income from the twelve books that I'd written during that time frame.

The Holy Spirit then whispered to me, *"God gave you wings so that you could fly, Red, and now it's time for you to use them."*

Wow, that was confirmation for me to take the plunge—sink or swim. I had to place my faith in God and pursue my writing full-time after that revelation, because faith without works is dead. Driving for Uber had been good to me, but it was time to take things to the next level. I then decided that it would be the last time I'd ever drive for Uber.

A Personal Note of Thanks

Thank you for taking the time to purchase and read *Night in the Underworld*. I would really love to hear from you, and it's customers like you who give me the inspiration to create urban fiction stories like this one. If you enjoyed reading the book, please leave an honest review at Amazon, and you can contact me for information about my current and upcoming books at: markstephenoneal@gmail.com

Made in the USA
Monee, IL
09 July 2022

99397487R00030